To Samuel
    from Gram and Grandpa
        Dague

Samuel's
1st Christmas and 1st Hanukkah
December 1994

CTW
SESAME STREET®
A GROWING-UP BOOK™

A Grouch's Christmas

By Michaela Muntean

Illustrated by Tom Leigh

Luis is played by Emilio Delgado

A SESAME STREET/GOLDEN PRESS BOOK

Published by Western Publishing Company, Inc., in conjunction with Children's Television Workshop.

It was the day before Christmas and Elmo was helping his mother make Christmas cookies. Elmo watched his mother roll the dough out on the countertop. Then he cut out shapes in the dough with cookie cutters and sprinkled them with colored sugar.

Soon the whole house was filled with the sweet smell of baking cookies. Elmo stood in front of the oven door and watched as the cookies turned golden brown.

When the cookies came out of the oven, Elmo's mother said, "You may try one, Elmo. But we have to save the rest for our Christmas guests. This year you are big enough to pass the plate of cookies yourself."

"And I will tell everyone that I helped make them,"
Elmo said as he picked out a reindeer-shaped cookie.
"These are good!" he said. "Cookie Monster will love
them."

As Elmo's mother was putting away the flour and sugar, she glanced out the kitchen window.

"Look, Elmo!" she said.

"It's snowing!" he cried. "May I please go outside to play?"

"Yes," said Elmo's mother. Then she helped him put on his coat and hat and boots. As she tied a big scarf around his neck she said, "Keep dry and don't stay out too long."

"Okay," Elmo said, and he ran out the door and down
Sesame Street to build a snowmonster. He saw the
footprints that his boots made in the new snow.

The snow was as white and fine as the flour Elmo's
mother sprinkled on the counter for the cookie dough.
Snowflakes drifted down and clung to Elmo's hat and
scarf. He opened his mouth to catch some more.

Elmo met Ernie and Bert carrying a Christmas tree.
"Merry Christmas!" said Elmo.
"Merry Christmas, Elmo!" Ernie and Bert answered.
All along Sesame Street, Elmo saw his friends getting
ready for Christmas. Luis was stringing colored lights
in the window of the Fix-It Shop. Big Bird was
decorating his nest with holly branches. Herry Monster
had dressed up like Santa Claus, and he was ringing a
bell and collecting toys and food for needy families.
The Count was counting snowflakes as they fell.
"Merry Christmas, everybody!" Elmo shouted.
"Merry Christmas, Elmo!" everybody called back.

"Merry Christmas, Oscar!" said Elmo as he passed Oscar's trash can.

"Humph!" said Oscar. "I hate Christmas!"

Elmo stopped suddenly. He lifted up the earflaps of his cap and said, "Would you please say that again, Oscar? I don't think I heard right."

"Of course I will," grumbled Oscar. "I'll say it again and again and again. I hate Christmas, I hate Christmas, I hate Christmas!"

"But how could you hate Christmas?" Elmo said. "There's nothing about Christmas to hate!"

"Oh, yes there is," said Oscar. "There's all that ho-ho-ho-ing and fa-la-la-ing. There's everyone going around smiling and being cheerful and giving each other nice presents. This is the worst time of year for grouches."

"Oh, Oscar!" said Elmo. "There are things about
Christmas even a grouch would like."

"Name one," said Oscar.

Elmo thought for a minute. "Cookies!" he said. "I just
helped my mommy make Christmas cookies."

"Were they sardine cookies with chocolate icing?"
Oscar asked.

"No," Elmo said. "They were sugar cookies shaped like
stars and Christmas trees and reindeer. I cut them out
all by myself!"

"Yucch," said Oscar. "They sound awful."

"Just wait!" said Elmo. "I'll be back! I'm going to find a *zillion* reasons for you to like Christmas!"

"Don't worry," said Oscar. "I'm not going anywhere until the holidays are over!" And he disappeared inside his trash can and slammed the lid down with a crash.

Elmo forgot all about building snowmonsters. He went looking for reasons for Oscar to like Christmas. If he couldn't find a zillion, he was sure he could find a few.

First Elmo stopped to visit Ernie and Bert. He told them what he wanted to do.

"I've got an idea!" said Ernie. "We'll meet you at Oscar's trash can in one hour."

Next Elmo stopped to see Big Bird, and he said he'd help, too. Then Elmo visited Luis and Herry and the Count. They all agreed to meet at Oscar's.

Elmo raced back home and told his mother what he
wanted to do.

"That sounds disgusting," she said. But she helped
anyway.

When everything was ready, Elmo hurried to Oscar's can. His friends were there, just as they had promised.

"Merry Christmas, Oscar!" Elmo called as he knocked on the trash can lid.

"I told you," Oscar cried, popping out of his can, "I hate Christmas."

"And I told you I was going to find a zillion reasons why you would like it," Elmo said.

"Did you?" Oscar asked.

"No," Elmo said. "But I found a few really good ones!"

"Here!" said Ernie and Bert, handing Oscar a little Christmas tree. It was decorated with old tin cans, orange peels, and bits of raggedy string.

"That's not a bad-looking Christmas tree," Oscar said.

"You see?" said Ernie. "That's one thing to like about Christmas, Oscar."

"The nice thing about Christmas trees is that you can decorate them any way you like," Bert said. "We decorated this one especially for you, Oscar."

"I like Christmas because it's a family time," said Big Bird. "Tomorrow my Granny Bird is coming to visit."

"So?" said Oscar.

"So maybe Grundgetta would come and visit you if you invited her," said Big Bird.

"Hmmm," said Oscar, "that's not the worst idea I've ever heard. Grundgetta and I could sit around complaining and grumbling."

"You see?" said Big Bird. "That's another nice thing about Christmas—families getting together and enjoying themselves."

"I like Christmas because it's about sharing and helping others. Today I collected toys and food for families who needed them," said Herry Monster.

"And tonight Maria and I are going to deliver them," said Luis. "You don't happen to have anything to share, do you, Oscar?"

"Just a minute," Oscar said as he disappeared into his trash can.

He came back a few seconds later. "Here," said Oscar as he handed Herry a brand-new red-and-white-striped scarf. "Maybe someone could use it."

"Why, thank you, Oscar!" said Herry. "I'm sure someone could. Doesn't it feel good to help someone else?"

"I suppose so," Oscar said with a shrug. "It sure feels good to get rid of that scarf. It's too clean and it doesn't have one moth hole in it. I wouldn't want Grundgetta to see it if she comes tomorrow."

"I made *twelve* reasons for you to like Christmas!"
said Elmo. "Here are a dozen sardine Christmas cookies
with chocolate icing. Merry Christmas, Oscar!"

"There is something else to like," said the Count.
"What's that?" asked Oscar.
"Your friends!" said the Count. "When you count your blessings, count your friends. Let me count them for you...."
"Never mind, Count!" said Oscar. "I can do it."

Oscar was quiet for a minute. Then he turned to Elmo. "Okay, I give up! You were right, Elmo. Christmas isn't so bad after all."

Then Oscar took a bite of a sardine cookie. "And these cookies are delicious. Thanks, Elmo. And Merry Christmas."

Then everybody began to sing, and Oscar sang the fa-la-la-ing part the loudest.